The Teeny Tiny

GHOST

by Kay Winters

illustrated by Lynn Munsinger

SCHOLASTIC INC.

New York Toronto London Auckland Sydney

Mexico City New Delhi Hong Kong

ISBN 0-439-13351-3

Text copyright © 1997 by Kay Winters. Illustrations copyright © 1997 by Lynn Munsinger. All rights reserved.

Published by Scholastic Inc., 555 Broadway, New York, NY 10012, by arrangement with HarperCollins Publishers.

SCHOLASTIC and associated logos are trademarks and/or registered trademarks of Scholastic Inc.

12 11 10 9 8 7 6 5 4 3 2 1   9/9 0 1 2 3 4/0

Printed in the U.S.A.   24

First Scholastic printing, September 1998

Typography by Elynn Cohen

For Wulf —L.M.

With love to my daughter,
Linda Winters, who is always
cheering me on.   —K.W.

With special thanks to
Amy Edgar and Katherine Tegen

Once there was a timid
teeny tiny ghost.
He lived in a teeny tiny house
with two teeny tiny black cats.

The teeny tiny ghost
went to Teeny Tiny School.

He learned his
teeny tiny alphabet,

shivered at spooky stories,
and heard about Halloween.
He had never been out on that night,
but it sounded very scary.

Each day after school
the teeny tiny ghost
tried to do his homework.
"Haunting is very hard,"
he told his teeny tiny black cats.
They sat on the windowsill to watch.

First he *booooooed*,
then he *whooooooed*,
till he made the rafters rumble

and he had to hide his teeny tiny head.

Then he *howwwwwled*
and he *yeowwwwwled*
till the echoes came a-calling

and he had to hide his teeny tiny head.

"I'll never learn,"
wailed the teeny tiny ghost.
"I'm so timid, I scare myself!"
And a teeny tiny tear
slid down his cheek.

His teeny tiny cats
climbed on his lap,
licked his teeny tiny face,
and *purr*red their teeny tiny purrs.

On Halloween night some eerie yellow lights

bobbed by the house of the teeny tiny ghost.

"What's that?" he said,
holding his cats close.
And his teeny tiny heart
beat *bumpety-bump*.

Then he heard *RAP TAP TAP*
on his teeny tiny door.
"*Whoooo's* there?"
called the teeny tiny ghost.

"Let us in," cried the voices,
and they sounded very big.

The teeny tiny ghost
looked around.
Could he hide?
He slipped inside the
grandfather clock.

But he shivered and shook
till he made the clock chime
BING ... BONG ...
BING ... BONG ...BING.

The teeny tiny ghost
thought his head would explode.
He undid the latch and escaped.

RAP TAP TAP
came the knocking
on his teeny tiny door.
"Let us in!" cried the voices,
and they sounded very loud!

The teeny tiny cats
*mewww*ed and *meowww*ed.
"Don't be afraid,"
said the teeny tiny ghost.
"I won't run away.
I'll keep you safe.
We have to be
very very brave."

The teeny tiny ghost
took a long large breath.
He *hufffed*
and he *pufffed*
till he felt very big.

He *boooed*,
and he *whoooed*,
till he felt very bold.
He *howwwwwled*,
then he *yeowwwwwled*,
and he sounded very loud.

Then he heard hands clapping,
and he heard voices cheering,
"Bravo! for the teeny tiny ghost."
"It's Halloween! Trick or treat!"
cried the ghosts from his school,
and they pranced about
in costumes and masks.

His best friend, Gilbert,
wore a blue sailor suit.
He tooted tiny tunes
on a teeny tiny horn.

His teeny tiny teacher
had a hat and cape.
"You can be a magician
with your teeny tiny cats!"

Then the teeny tiny ghost
and his teeny tiny friends
sailed up the street on parade.

They tapped on teeny windows,
they rapped on tiny doors,
while jack-o'-lanterns smiled
in the bat-black night.

The teeny tiny ghost
gave a teeny tiny giggle
and whispered to his teeny tiny cats:

"HAPPY HALLOWEEN!"